This is my rock.

Not your rock.

This is my rock.

Not your rock.

This is my rock.

Not your rock.

This is my rock.

Not your rock.

GO... AWAY!

Hmm...
What now?

Yodel-odel-odel-odelay-hee-hoo!

clippity
cloppity
clippity
clip!
tippity
tappity
tippity
tap!

Hmm... Hungry.

Brrr... Cold.

Alone.

Hello little bird.

I know!

See that rock?
Your rock?
Our rock.

Actually this is MY rock.
I'll race you to the top.